Schoolies™

Making Friends

Based on the characters created by
Ellen Crimi-Trent

priddy books

Leeza was a very loud Schoolie.
Her twin sister Lydia, was a shy Schoolie.

Hi, I'm Leeza!
I'm Lydia.

At school, when Leeza sat with her friends,
Lydia felt too shy to join them.

One day, Mrs. Meow told the Schoolies that it was Friendship Week. This was a special week all about friendship.

Friendship Week
Can anyone tell me how to be a good friend?
Share!
1 +1 =2
Be helpful!
Be kind!

Lydia drooped.
She felt too shy to be friendly.

Mrs. Meow set a jar on her desk.
She called it the Friendship Jar.

Drop a note into the jar whenever another Schoolie acts friendly!

Lydia drooped a bit more.
She didn't think that she would get
any notes in the Friendship Jar.

At lunch, Lydia took an empty seat beside Spencer.

Lydia noticed Spencer wasn't eating.
She straightened up and spoke,
but no louder than a whisper.

Are you okay?
I forgot my lunch.

Lydia opened her lunch box,
and offered to share.

Sandwich?
Thanks!

Tomorrow it'll be my turn to share.

After eating lunch, they decided they would sit together again.

At recess, Lydia sat alone, beneath her favorite tree, to read her favorite book.

BAM! The tree shook,
and leaves fell.

Poor Zippy, the fastest Schoolie at Angler Elementary, had crashed into Lydia's tree!

Are you okay?
Ow! My head hurts!

Lydia took Zippy to see Mrs. Fox, the school nurse.

Then it was time for music class.
Mrs. Hedge played piano while the Schoolies played musical instruments or sang.

Hayden couldn't follow the beat on his drum.

Lydia clapped in time to the beat so Hayden could follow along.

Try this!
Oh, now I get it!

Soon Hayden was tapping his drum
in time to the music.

Lydia's happy heart seemed to beat in time to the music. She began to sing.

Everyone heard a wonderful voice.

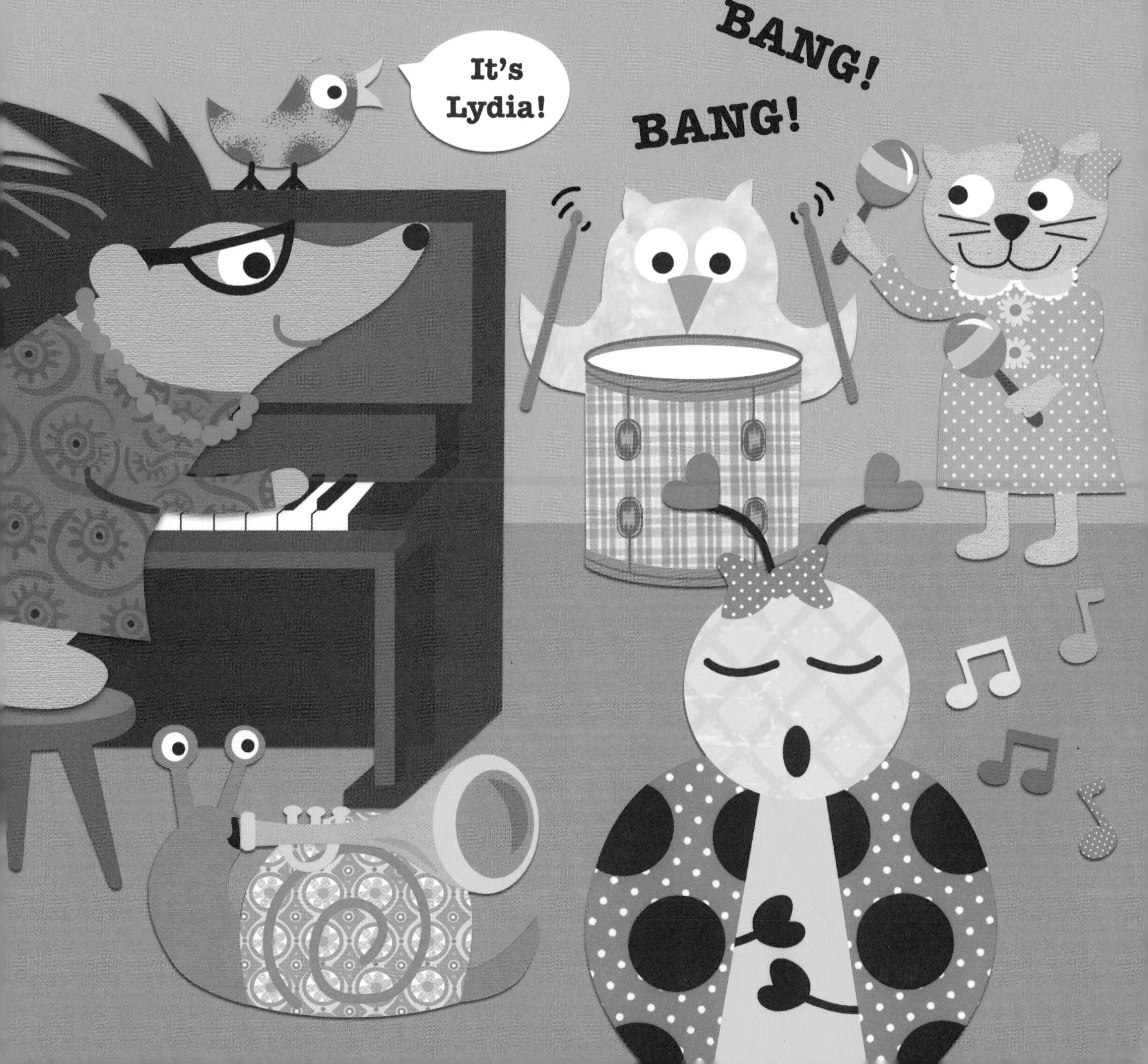
It's Lydia!
BANG!
BANG!

At the end of the day, Mrs. Meow was surprised to see so many notes in the Friendship Jar.

What's this? Friendship week has only just begun!

Mrs. Meow read the notes out loud.
They were all for Lydia!

Lydia is kind.
Lydia shares.
Lydia is helpful.

Lydia blushed. She smiled, and in a quiet, but very clear voice, she spoke.

Thank you, friends!